KILLING FOR LUXURY

© Aladdin Books Ltd 1992

Designed and produced by
Aladdin Books Ltd
28 Percy Street
London W1P 9FF

First published in
Great Britain in 1992 by
Franklin Watts Ltd
96 Leonard Street
London EC2A 4RH

ISBN 0 7496 0767 X

A CIP catalogue record for this book is available from the British Library.

Printed in Belgium

The original edition of this title was published in the **Survival** series.

The front cover photograph shows an African elephant, an endangered species often poached for its ivory tusks.

The author, Michael Bright, is a Senior Producer at the BBC's Natural History Unit, Bristol, UK. He is also the author of many books on Natural History.

Contents

KILLING FOR LUXURY

Michael Bright

Franklin Watts

London : New York : Toronto : Sydney

Introduction

Man has always killed animals. The killing was traditionally for food and clothing, but a carcass also provided household utensils, jewellery and other adornments. Nothing was wasted; all the parts were used. Today, however, many millions of animals are killed each year – not to provide essential food for survival but to supply a profitable luxury market. Some animals are killed to furnish the well-off with status symbols, but what price do animals pay to satisfy this vanity? Certain animals are reared in captivity solely for their fur, their skin, or a scent they produce. Is this an acceptable way to obtain an animal product? In some cases, hunting has also become a luxury.

Many of the wild animals traded in the luxury market are in danger of extinction. Clearly they must be protected. But sometimes there is a dilemma. Who should have priority – native people who need to kill even rare animals in order to survive, or the rare animal species themselves? The Convention on International Trade in Endangered Species of Wild Fauna and Flora (CITES) exists to control the world trade in animal products. Still, though, many species are killed and traded illegally. Some, like elephants and rhinos, are endangered. The sea mink, exploited for its fur, is now extinct. How many more species will disappear before we insist that the killing must stop?

▷ The baby harp seal has a highly prized white coat for the first six weeks of its life. Hunters once killed 120,000 baby seals each year for their fur. This slaughter has now ended, thanks to a public outcry. However, Norwegian hunters still take white seal coats. It is estimated they may have killed up to 25,000 harp seals since the 1983 ban.

△ Eskimos (Inuit) also kill seals for fur and food. This is a traditional hunt, and the hunters have great respect for the hunted. They take only what they need and no more.

Trapping for fur

Behind the elegant facade of the multimillion dollar fashion fur industry is the reality of the killing. Every year, millions of trapped animals suffer a slow and painful death. They are caught by the leg, neck or body in metal traps or nooses. Each animal is held in its trap for an average of 15 hours before it is strangled or bludgeoned to death by the trapper. One Alaskan lynx remained trapped by the leg for six weeks. It stayed alive for so long because others in its family brought it food. The traps are indiscriminate. Many non-target animals, such as eagles, owls, swans and domestic pets, are caught, killed and discarded. These are known in the trade as "trash" animals.

Fur Fashion
In the United States the retail trade in furs, despite the anti-fur campaigns, has tripled during the past decade to a $2 billion industry. Men's fashion accounts for much of the increase. More and more people can afford real and expensive furs and feel it is morally acceptable to buy them. The American Fur Association says about 10 per cent of furs come from wild animals.

▽ The most commonly used trap in North America is the leghold or gin trap. The two metal jaws spring shut when an animal stands on the trip mechanism. It is like having a car door slammed on your hand. The flesh of the animal's leg is often cut and the bones broken. Sometimes a desperate animal will gnaw off its own foot in an attempt to get free.

▷ Thousands of red foxes like the one opposite are killed across Europe for their fur. Many are trapped, snared or poisoned illegally by "cowboy" hunters. Protected badgers are also caught by mistake sometimes.

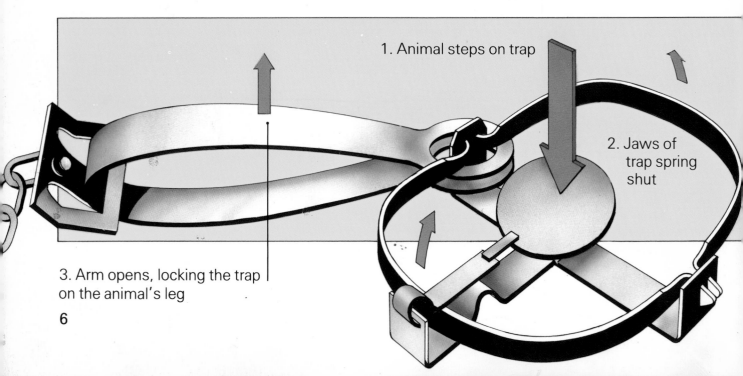

1. Animal steps on trap

2. Jaws of trap spring shut

3. Arm opens, locking the trap on the animal's leg

▷ This is an image used by the British animal rights group LYNX in their anti-fur campaign.

In the lands bordering the Arctic, people depend on fur trapping for their living. Many fear that a ban on trapping could seriously affect the isolated Canadian Indian and Inuit communities of this area. Others believe that trapping is further justified because it keeps the population of fur-bearing animals under control.

Some countries condemn trapping yet still import skins. For example, of the millions of skins imported into Britain each year, many are still from animals trapped in the wild by gin traps – devices which were banned in Britain in 1956 after a government report described them as "diabolical instruments which cause an incalculable amount of suffering".

Fur ranching

"I've never quite understood the notion that wearing a dead animal is attractive. I have absolutely no desire to wear a fur and have never owned one. I would always prefer to see the fur on the animal."

Marie Helvin, Model

Most furs are not from animals caught in the wild. They come from fur ranches, where large numbers of animals like mink, sable and fox are reared in small cages. Fur ranching or farming is big business. In Norway, more than 2,000 fur farms accounted for 22% of Scandinavian production in 1991. Norway now supplies 18% of the world's furs.

Production has gone up four-fold in the past decade, despite pressure from anti-fur campaigners. The fact is that in most parts of the world, a real fur coat is still regarded as a status symbol. In Texas, people can be seen wearing expensive furs even on a hot sunny day. In northern climes, however, people still regard fur coats as the best insulation against the cold.

△ This Arctic fox is in a small cage on a fur farm in the north of England. It must be kept alone or it will fight and kill its cell mates. It walks on a wire floor so wastes fall through and do not damage its precious coat. It will die either by electrocution, lethal injection or gassing.

△ Vicuna like the ones above are a type of llama found in Chile and Peru. Once they were abundant, but their numbers were considerably reduced after the Spanish invaders began to kill the animals for their highly-prized wool. Traditionally the Incas (the people living in Peru before the arrival of the Spanish) had sheared vicuna without killing them. Today, hunting and killing vicuna for their wool is banned. Instead the herds are rounded up on protected mountain "ranches" and sheared in the traditional way.

Fur farmers consider that fur farming is the acceptable face of the fur industry. They claim that their animals are in excellent health and in good condition. If they were not, they say, the pelts would become mangy and lose value.

The animals are kept in small cages with wire floors and no outside runs. This is because the farmers are afraid that the animals would dirty and damage their fur if left outside. Nevertheless, pelts do get damaged due to fighting, urine contamination or bad nutrition, and this causes huge financial loss to the fur farms. Nor do the animals confined to cages always remain intact. Mink are aggressive and bite one another. Sometimes they fall victim to cannibalism.

In the firing line

Many of nature's great hunters have become the hunted. Poachers shoot, trap and poison some of the rarest animals in the world just to provide exclusive fur coats for the luxury market. The skins of spotted cats, for example, command high prices, and this encourages illegal hunting. Sometimes, legal trade makes the situation worse. Skins of protected species, declared before the introduction of restrictions, are allowed to be sold even after a ban. This legitimate trade often hides further poaching and illegal dealings. For example, many of India's spotted cats, such as the snow leopard, are illegally hunted down by nomadic tribesmen. The animals are killed in the Himalayas and their pelts are smuggled down to Kashmir where they are sold alongside legally acquired skins or smuggled further to Europe or Japan.

In other parts of the world, polar bears, wolves, kangaroos, tigers, seals and zebra all lose their skins to hunters. Even pelts of the extremely rare giant panda, the very symbol of conservation, have been discovered in an illegal trade from China to Taiwan.

"We no longer eat other people's brains to acquire wisdom; are we still primitive enough to wear animals' skins to achieve beauty?"

Joanna Lumley, Actress and writer

◁ The cheetah, seen in the picture on the left, is still a target for illegal hunting. There are about 10,000 left in Africa, and a small number in Iran.

▽ Many of the spotted cats are fully protected, yet very expensive fur coats are still made from their skins. On sale are leopard skins from Africa and China, snow leopard from Asia, and ocelot, jaguar, tiger cat and margay from South America. They are all readily available in fashion stores in Munich and Tokyo. One year after a ban on the export of spotted cat skins from Paraguay to Germany, 95,000 pelts were traded.

The legal fur markets of Europe handle 700,000 pelts from wild animals each year. Two-thirds are the skins of small spotted cats. The illegal trade may be even greater. Traders have discovered ways and means of concealing the source and destination of illegal skins by channelling them through third party countries where they acquire legal international trade documents. This process is called "laundering".

Other ways of cheating the system include giving false declarations of species' names, country of origin and purpose of import. A few years ago, a large shipment of cheetah skins was intercepted at Hong Kong's Kai Tak airport on a flight from Switzerland. The consignment was labelled "Italian mink".

Big cats

The big cats (lion, tiger, leopard, jaguar, snow leopard, clouded leopard and cheetah) and small cats (lynx, bobcat, puma, ocelot and several species, such as the serval and caracal) are all carnivores. They are successful predators at the top of their food chains and have few predators themselves, apart from man. However, the large scale slaughter of tigers and ocelots and the trade in their patterned skins brought them almost to extinction. As a result tigers became a protected species in 1972. Since then their numbers have begun to increase again.

▽ The leopard in the photograph below is from India. Leopards are found throughout southern Asia and across Africa, making them the most widespread members of the cat family. Leopards are solitary animals. They hunt at night, ambushing prey or stalking very closely with considerable stealth. Prey is taken into a tree where it is out of the reach of lions and hyenas.

The leopard
Male leopards may be up to 190cm long, have a 100cm tail, stand 80cm at the shoulder and weigh some 90kg. Females are about half that size. They live for about 12 years in the wild and up to 20 years in captivity.

▷ The colour and fur pattern of the spotted cats varies with habitat. The basic background colour is brown, grey, or golden yellow with darker circles or rosettes.

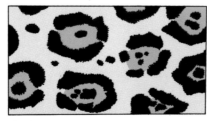

△ Jaguar

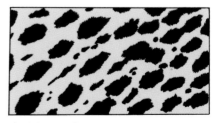

△ Cheetah

The lynx
Adult lynx can be over a metre long, stand 75cm at the shoulder and weigh up to 38kg. They live for 12-15 years. North American bobcats differ from lynx in having dark spots, bare feet and no ear tufts.

△ The brownish-grey colour of the lynx allows it to blend into the background in a dense coniferous forest.

It lives in the cold northern latitudes in Scandinavia, across northern Asia and in some parts of North America.

It can travel on long legs through deep snow. The foot pads are insulated with thick fur. It has ear tufts.

◁ The snow leopard lives in the mountains of southern Asia. It has long and very thick winter fur. Little is known of its habits. It is nocturnal, solitary and shy.

The snow leopard
Large individuals grow to 130cm in length. The tail is 100cm long. They stand about 60cm at the shoulder and weigh up to 75kg. They live to about 15 years in captivity.
It is also known as the mountain panther.

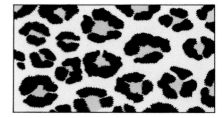

△ Leopard

△ Snow leopard

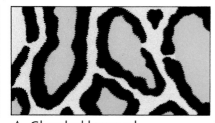

△ Clouded leopard

Skinned for leather

Cows and pigs are not the only animals used to provide leather. Snakes, crocodiles, kangaroos, caiman, lizards and sharks are all slaughtered and their hides turned into fashionable shoes and clothes. Some of this trade is legal; but much of it is not. In 1986 El Salvador exported 134,000 caiman skins, despite having a caiman population of only 10,000. The "extra" skins came from countries where there is a restriction on trade, such as Panama and Colombia.

Caiman killing has become like a military operation. Helicopter gun-ships fly over remote lakes and rivers at night. Searchlights locate the animals, which are shot between the eyes to avoid marking the skins. The next morning the follow-up party arrives to recover the bodies. These activities are illegal but, unfortunately, the poachers are better organised than the government control agencies.

▽ Sharks provide the toughest leather known. Many are caught by fishermen from Mexico (bottom left) who send the dried skins (bottom right) to the United States for tanning. In the past, it was used by furniture makers to rub down wood and swordsmen put it on sword handles to stop their hands slipping on the blood. Today, it is used to make quality shoes and cowboy boots. The trade is unrestricted and there are still a lot of sharks left in the sea. There is some concern, however, because many species of sharks have few offspring and live in fixed territories. Intensive fishing could very quickly wipe out an entire stock.

"The deliberate killing of any living creature from a shellfish to an elephant, not because anyone is hungry or cold, or would be ill without the product but merely for luxury or adornment, is morally unacceptable."

Richard Adams, author of "Watership Down"

One problem with trying to restrict trade in reptile skins is that the consumer countries in effect form a pact to ignore international controls. The primary importers of reptile skins (France, Japan, Italy and Germany) receive millions of hides each year, mostly from Asia and South America. Italy re-exports 90 per cent of its tanned hides, many to the United States.

Some countries have introduced crocodile farming to meet the demand for crocodile leather goods. The recognisable pattern on real skins is considered chic. But conservationists argue that the trade encourages illegal killing in the wild. When it comes to monitoring the trade, how do the customs authorities distinguish a farmed skin from a poached one anyway? Papua New Guinea's answer is to tag the farmed skins.

△ The handbags in the photograph above are made from the skins of monitor lizards. They are smuggled to Japan from Bangladesh, Indonesia and Pakistan. Snake skins are also popular, although the distinct skin patterns of pythons are easily spotted by customs agents. Simple but ingenious methods are employed to make illegal shipments. In a consignment of 400 tins of cashew nuts bound for Singapore from India, only 140 contained nuts. The rest housed snake skins worth $1.6 million.

Crocodiles

The crocodiles, alligators, caiman and gharials lived through the great extinctions that saw the dinosaurs disappear about 65 million years ago. They have survived virtually unchanged. But in just a hundred years, man has nearly wiped them all out. The crocodilians have large brains. As well as showing instinctive behaviour, they are capable of learning. They are well-adapted as aquatic predators with eyes and nostrils set on top of the head. This enables them to see and breathe at the surface with the body submerged.

The spectacled caiman
This South American caiman grows to over two metres from the snout to the tip of the tail. It lives in the Amazon and Orinoco river basins. Individuals grow about 30cm a year, and may live for 75 to 100 years if left alone by man.

△ The spectacled caiman, seen in the photograph above, is named for the horny ridge connecting the eye sockets. It resembles the bridge of a pair of spectacles. An adult caiman feeds on giant aquatic snails, piranha and any animal that strays within its range.

Caiman spend the day hiding in the reeds or basking in the sun on river banks. They hunt at night. Researchers count caiman by going out at night with a flashlight and spotting the reflections from their eyes. Poachers use the same technique.

Of the two million crocodilian skins traded legally each year, three-quarters are spectacled caiman. Another one million are smuggled from Paraguay, Bolivia and Brazil. Most are sent to Italy where they are turned into handbags or expensive wallets.

The Nile crocodile
Individuals can grow up to 6.5 metres long and weigh about 1,080kg. They live for over 50 years in the wild. Large ones are known to live for over a hundred years. Nile crocodiles account for many human deaths every year.

◁ This skin is from a saltwater crocodile, the largest of the crocodiles. Giants reach over six metres in length. They live along the coasts of southern Asia and north Australia, killing many people each year.

△ The Nile crocodile lives on the banks of rivers throughout Africa. The mother crocodile buries her eggs in the sand and guards the nest while they incubate. The youngsters hatch and call to the mother to dig them out. She then carries them in her mouth to the water. They live in nurseries in quiet back-waters for their first three months. If danger threatens, the mother gives a grunt and, all together, they dive below the surface of the water for safety.

Beauty and cruelty

Wildlife has always provided humans with the ingredients for medicines, potions, perfumes and cosmetics. Millions of animals have died in the mistaken belief that parts of their bodies have magical properties that can cure diseases, heal wounds, or enhance a person's appearance or desirability. People still seek those properties today. Traditions are difficult to change – especially when large profits are involved.

Luxury cosmetics are big business worldwide. But, increasingly, there is a strong public pressure against exploiting animals for frivolous purposes. Many people consider this use of animals unacceptable particularly now that synthetic products can replace animal ones. One successful cosmetics company has created an entire line without using animal products or testing their products on animals.

▽ Many people demand a halt to cosmetics testing on animals, and a halt to the killing of wild animals for the raw materials they provide. The musk deer has been particularly affected by its use in the cosmetics industry. Found in Siberia, China and Tibet, the animal is now being more carefully protected.

○ Musk glands (male only)
● Other scent glands

One animal caught in the clash between wildlife conservation and the cosmetics industry is the male musk deer. Poachers kill the deer for the musk gland, which contains one of the most valuable of wildlife products. The gland is cut out and dried. Some are used in perfumes, although substitutes are available. The rest have medicinal uses – "stamina" drinks, children's tonics, sedatives for the treatment of asthma and epilepsy, stimulants for bronchitis and pneumonia and as an aphrodisiac. In India traditional doctors use it as an effective heart and nerve stimulant and to help treat snake bites. Deer have been bred in captivity and their glands "milked", but the secretions produced in this way are inferior. The killing of musk deer to provide for the musk trade threatens the survival of the animal.

△ These jars contain tears from young dugongs, or sea cows. After the mothers are killed for meat, the young are kept alive and their tears collected. The liquid is sold to bring good luck, prosperity and success in love.

▽ Oil from civets like this one is used in medicines and perfumes. Although it can be extracted without killing the animal, civets are often shot or die from mishandling.

Horns and ivory

In Africa and Asia poaching has nearly wiped out all five species of rhinoceros. During the past two decades numbers have been reduced by 85 per cent. The horn, which is simply matted hair, is sought by Yemeni men for dagger handles and by makers of traditional medicines in the Far East to reduce a fever. Some people even take it as an aphrodisiac (a potion which is supposed to increase sexual desire). It is said to be worth its weight in gold. However, tests have shown that rhino horn has no medicinal value and is no better than eating your own nail clippings. Although Saiga antelope horn is offered as a substitute, the demand for rhino horn remains and the future of the species looks bleak.

▽ The park rangers in the photograph below are removing the horn from a rhino that died in a fight. The horn is stored by the government to prevent it being traded. In spite of these precautions, some do reach the market. The horn from a very rare African black rhino (bottom left) was seen in a Singapore medicine shop. A poacher will receive about $100/kg, while the same horn in North Yemen might be sold for $600/kg. There are about 11,000 rhinos left in Africa and about 3,000 in Asia.

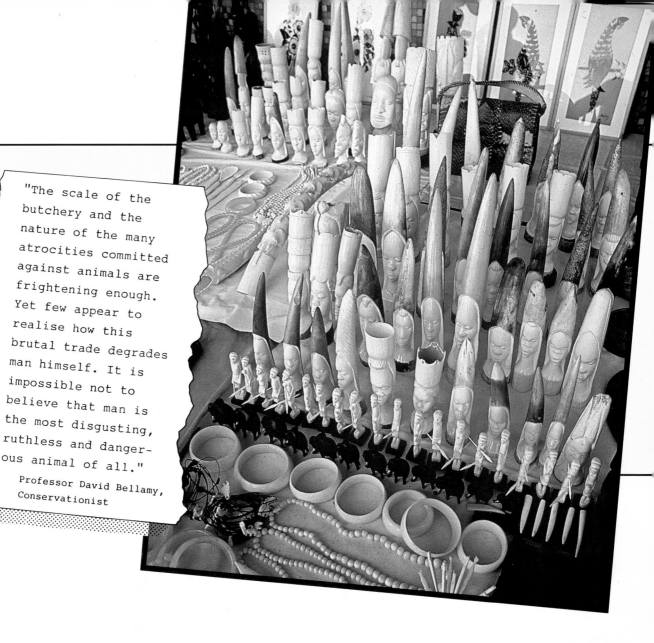

Ivory from elephants' tusks was so valuable that in some countries it was used as a currency instead of money. In the search for ivory in Africa, for example, whole elephant groups are slaughtered with sophisticated automatic weapons. Others die slowly and painfully from poisoned arrows. Only their tusks are valuable — their unwanted carcasses are left to rot.

Over 1,000 tonnes of raw ivory are traded each year. This represents the tusks of 70,000 elephants, many of them poached in Africa. Much of the ivory reaches Japan and Hong Kong, where it is carved into curios or hoarded as an investment. If the elephant becomes extinct the high price of the tusks will rocket even further.

△ The polished tusks and ivory statues and jewellery in the photograph above were spotted in a shop in Gabon, West Africa. Japan, however, is the world's largest consumer of ivory. In recent years, much of the ivory imported has been of poor quality. As the wild elephant populations dwindle, the well-organised poaching gangs are killing any animal they find — even baby elephants with peg-like tusks. In war zones, ivory is offered in exchange for weapons.

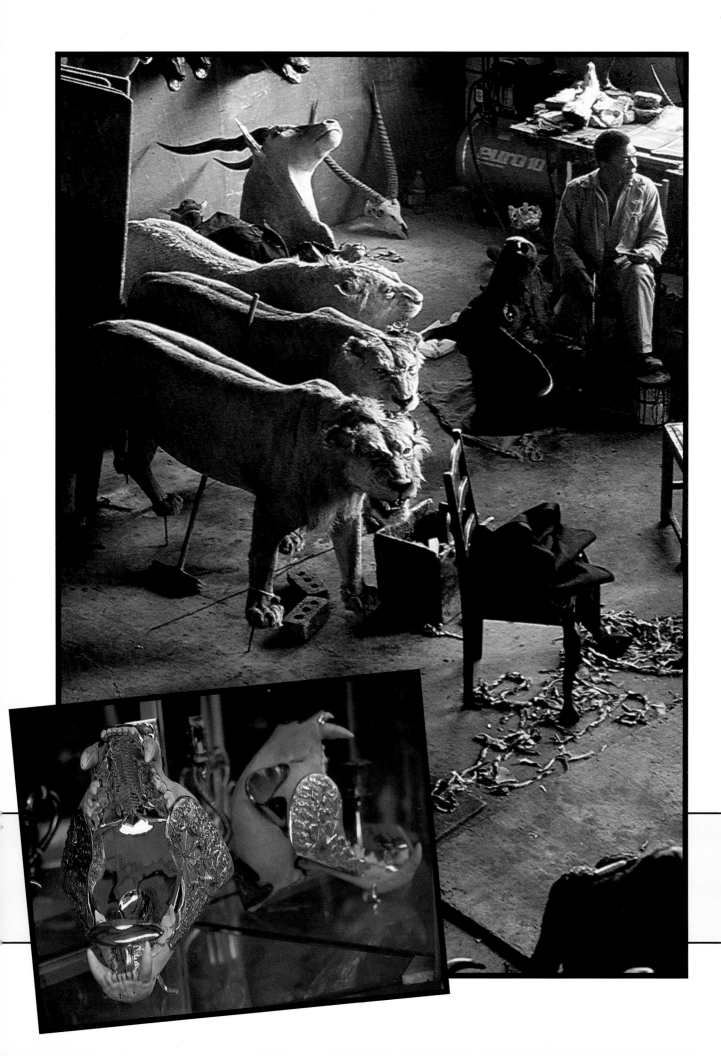

Trophies and curios

◁ The trade in wildlife curios, like those in the photograph on the left, is enormous. US imports alone amount to 130 million legal items a year. US officials annually seize illegal imports valued at more than $7 million. These include stuffed animals and skins, ivory products, shells and corals from South-east Asia, Hawaii and the Seychelles, Taiwanese butterflies, sponges from the Mediterranean and the Caribbean, and farmed ostrich-skin handbags made in Japan.

◁ The ashtray in the photograph on the left was seen in Bangkok. It is made from a tiger skull.

In most parts of the world, including Europe and the USA, wild animal products are still bought as status symbols and displayed in the home to impress friends and neighbours. Some people deliberately seek to possess parts of rare or dangerous animals to satisfy a "man-in-the wild" or "Rambo" image. Others buy curios innocently, unaware of the suffering involved. The heads of gorillas, for example, are hacked off, stuffed and mounted. Often it is the dominant male that is killed. Without his influence, group structure breaks down and the rest of his family will be likely to die too.

The range of curios is bizarre and varied. A gorilla's hand for an ashtray, an elephant's foot for a seat, a tiger's skin for a rug, or a stuffed rare leopard cat on the coffee-table are just some of the curios on offer. Smaller ornaments are often sold as souvenirs, such as a table napkin ring wrapped in lizard skin or a necklace made from sharks' teeth.

Sometimes the need for a wildlife product is legitimised. France claims that it needs to import large quantities of turtle shells to make spectacles for people who are allergic to synthetic products. But is this simply a disguise for a luxury market? In Japan, turtle-shell spectacles sell at $3,000 a pair.

"We have proof that drug smuggling and the illegal wildlife trade is controlled by the same Latin American Mafia."

Manfred Niekisch, TRAFFIC (wildlife trade monitoring unit) Germany

◁ This caged badger at a market in the Far East is destined for a cooking pot in a specialty restaurant. It is kept alive so that the restaurant can serve its meat fresh. Badgers are only one of many exotic animals that find their way onto menus of establishments specialising in unusual foods. In Africa, restaurants for wealthy tourists offer lion meat.

Luxury food

Inuit, who have a wide choice of foods to eat, harpoon very rare bowhead whales, store the meat, and eat it at Thanksgiving and Christmas. Is this "traditional" hunt (using modern firearms) necessary for their survival, or has it become a luxury? All over the world, the emphasis of traditional subsistence hunting has changed and wildlife has become a major ingredient in the exotic food trade for bored gourmets. Whale meat excites palates in Japan, Norway and Iceland. In Germany, many unusual animals can be bought at the butchers – elephant, tiger, puma, bear, python, crocodile, tapir and leopard.

△ Turtles are reared on farms (above) for their meat, which makes delicious soups. To keep them fresh, they are often left for hours on their backs. Most wild species are under threat, and it is argued that farming only encourages the poaching of wild turtles.

The huge demand for unusual foods has an enormous toll on wildlife. In certain luxury restaurants in Macao and Hong Kong, the rich can impress their friends with an illegal and cruel feast. A young monkey is brought to the table and strapped in a cage with its head protruding from the top. The cage is put under a table with the monkey's head sticking out from a hole in the centre. Its live brains are then eaten.

Europeans and Americans consider this ritual cruel. But their concept of cruelty is not universal. Different cultures have widely ranging views on how to treat animals. People outside Europe or North America may well consider boiling lobsters alive or eating frogs' legs to be unnecessarily cruel, or they may be alarmed by overfishing of the sea which can wipe out an entire species.

All the birds of the air

Birds have always been exploited for food. They are easy to spot and catch, and many species exist in large numbers. In Europe, the shooting of song birds was a traditional way to supplement peasant diets. There was little impact on bird populations. Today, however, many birds end up in luxury restaurants where delicacies like pickled skylark and thrush pâté are in great demand and the hunt has become a massacre. Hundreds of millions of birds migrating from Africa to Europe are killed each spring. They are shot, mist-netted, spring-trapped or caught on sticky lime perches. The killing is indiscriminate, sometimes for food but often for fun. Spain accounts for 30 million deaths a year, France and Italy 40 million each. Malta, Cyprus, Lebanon, Portugal and Greece also take their toll.

In south-west France, the turtle-dove shoot mobilises tens of thousands of hunters. They sit on raised platforms and pick off the migrating doves, not heeding the laws banning the cull. An EC Directive on Conservation of Wild Birds requires member states to protect all migrants. The strong hunting lobby along the Mediterranean ensures that the ban is ignored.

"In my opinion, wanton and casual destruction of wildlife is an offence not only against Nature, but against civilisation."

Bill Oddie,
Entertainer and
birdwatcher

▽ The starling in the photograph is tied to the stick as a lure. As it flaps about, it attracts other birds which are trapped and killed. The flock of starlings (below right) were caught when they dropped down to investigate such a decoy in northern Italy.

There are several examples in the recent past of the large scale slaughter of birds leading to the destruction of the species. The North American passenger pigeon was probably the world's most numerous bird. Hundreds of millions thrived in huge flocks that filled the sky. They were hunted relentlessly for food and sport, until the last one died in 1914. Today habitat destruction is reducing the numbers of many species. Indiscriminate shooting may push them over the edge into extinction.

△ These chicks are cave swiftlets from Malaysia. They sit in a nest made partly from the dried saliva of the parents. It is the main ingredient of an expensive delicacy, birds' nest soup. Only deserted nests are supposed to be taken but often collectors tip chicks out to gain their prize. The chicks are then torn apart on the cave floor by voracious insects.

"Most of the species of mammals and birds which are killed by hunting and shooting still exist in larger numbers than would be the case if these sports were to be eliminated."
Professor Kenneth Mellanby, former Director of Terrestrial Ecology, UK

Hunter and the hunted

Different cultures have a variety of attitudes to the killing of wildlife. For some it is simply for food. For others it is a means of getting rich quickly or maintaining important traditions. In North America and northern Europe it is for the sheer thrill of the kill itself, and the shooting of bears, wolves, deer and elk in the USA is big business. In Scotland, hunters stalk stags for their antlers – a sport which is very profitable. These hunters have no interest in taking part in the less glamorous cull of the female deer. Consequently, the herds have become unbalanced, with too many deer searching for food. But shooters also breed game animals, releasing them back into the wild, and then shooting them. This kind of hunting often takes place on large estates which preserve the wilderness area.

In affluent Europe and North America the species hunted are not usually endangered. But in other parts of the world taking from the wild is a necessary way of life. Why should the poor care about a species' extinction when they have to be more concerned about their own survival? But unscrupulous dealers, lured by cash from the West, take advantage of their plight and encourage the plunder of the wild. Until the customers realise the damage caused to satisfy their whims and desires, the wild world will continue to be ravaged.

◁ To track a deer in the forest and shoot it with a bow and arrow (left) requires skill and patience. In some people hunting and shooting appears to satisfy a primitive urge to stalk and to kill. Hunting is popular. In Canada, for example, the annual hunt of migratory wildfowl is eagerly awaited by about 400,000 sharpshooters. However, they also help the environment because part of the permit fee is donated to Wildlife Habitat Canada.

Hard facts

The three animals listed below are in particular danger because of poaching for the luxury market.

Leopard
These animals may be doing better than expected. There are over 700,000 leopards in Africa south of the Sahara. It was recommended that they still be protected but that controlled hunting be allowed. Conservationists are sceptical.

Rhinoceros
Africa's rhino population has dropped from 100,000, 25 years ago, to 11,000 today. They are disappearing at the rate of one animal per day.

Elephant
There are 3,760,000 elephants left in Africa. The numbers have halved in the last ten years. In 1986, the tusks of 89,000 elephants, worth $50M, were traded illegally.

China and Hong Kong
A clouded leopard might fall into a pit trap set for it on mainland China. It will then be sold illegally to, for example, a Hong Kong restaurant for a massive price. The animal is prepared for the table in a very particular way. It is placed in a secure cage, dropped into water and drowned. The leopard's body is simmered for four hours and is then served hot to about 14 oriental gourmets.

European Community
A ban on steel-toothed traps in EC countries begins in 1993. In 1995, the EC is to introduce a ban on furs from animals caught in cruel traps, imported from non-EC countries.

▽ This is a colobus monkey mother with her baby. These African primates are killed in great numbers for their fur.

There is a huge trade in animal products for a luxury market in the following countries. Often the killing itself occurs outside the country named.

Australia, Mozambique and Malawi
Not all crocodiles and alligators are fully protected and, as a result, many species have suffered a rapid decline in populations. These three countries want to lower the protection afforded their crocodilians. Australia wishes to cull its saltwater crocodiles and Malawi and Mozambique want to hunt their Nile crocodiles and cash in on the profitable trade.

Burundi
This African nation exported 50,000 tusks in 1986. It has no elephant population of its own.

France and French Guyana
Skins and other wildlife products from protected species, such as caiman, sea turtles and spotted cats, find their way illegally from Surinam and Brazil into French Guyana and then to the international market place.

Greece
Low taxes and labour costs and a booming tourist trade have combined to create a profitable market for cheap furs. There are 200 fur shops on the small island of Rhodes alone. In Athens in 1991, 16 out of 22 fur shops in the city were selling illegal spotted cat fur coats.

India, Indonesia and Bangladesh

These three countries supply most of the 11,000 tonnes of frogs' legs traded in the world annually. Indonesia is the main supplier to the EC, and Bangladesh to the USA. India has taken the lead in controlling trade by issuing licences to those who stun the frogs with electricity before severing the legs. Elsewhere legs are sliced off living frogs.

Japan

Since 1985, over 10 tonnes of caiman skins entered Japan illegally. They have also imported hawksbill turtle shell, saltwater crocodile skins and musk from Indonesia. Under pressure from the USA, Japan is to ban the import of turtle shell as of 1993.

Kenya

In July, 1991, the Kenyan government ceremonially burned 6.8 tonnes of ivory to protest against poaching.

However, chimpanzee skulls mounted on carvings of human figures are being sold on Nairobi roadside stalls for $250-400. The skulls are imported from Zaire, Uganda and Tanzania, where the chimpanzee is officially classified as endangered.

Malaysia

Logging and the gourmet food trade are both threatening Malaysia's protected wildlife. Turtles and snakes are made into soups, while monkey brains and meat, flying squirrels, bats and deer are popular as main courses.

Malta

Between 2-3 million birds are shot on Malta every year. Of those, about 50,000 are birds of prey, like hobbies. Hobbies are protected on Malta but are shot anyway, stuffed and added to shooters' collections. Some collections contain over 250 birds.

Namibia

Cape fur seals on the coast of Namibia are culled annually. The 1991 quota is 25,400 animals, of which 23,400 are pups and 2,000 are adult seals. South Africa is considering a cull of 140,000 cape fur seals.

North America

Many of North America's 90,000 bobcat skins (from trapped animals) are exported to Europe, particularly to Germany, as are most of the 14,000 lynx skins.

South America

A substance which looks and feels like ivory can be obtained from the nut of a South American tropical rainforest palm tree called the tagua. Every year one tree can produce enough nuts to equal the amount of ivory from an elephant's tusks.

Worldwide

The illegal international trade in wildlife is still big business. It is worth over $1.5 billion. Each year 50,000 live primates, ivory from 70,000 African elephants, 4 million live birds, 10 million reptile skins, and 350 million tropical fish are bought and sold worldwide.

Zimbabwe

This African nation has introduced more intense anti-poaching patrols to protect its 500 black rhinos, the world's largest viable population. These patrols include a World Wide Fund for Nature helicopter to seek out gangs of organised poachers.

Useful addresses
Friends of the Earth
26-28 Underwood Street
London N1 7JQ

Greenpeace
Canonbury Villas
London N1 2PN

World Wide Fund for Nature
Panda House
Weyside Park
Godalming, Surrey GU7 1XR

Young People's Trust for Endangered Species
95 Woodbridge Road
Guildford
Surrey GU1 4PY

Index

Photographic Credits:
Cover and pages 4-5, 5, 7, 13 (both), 14 (both), 15, 16, 17 (right), 18, 19 (bottom), 20, 21, 22 (inset), 26 (both) and 28: Bruce Coleman; pages 9 and 10: Planet Earth; pages 7 and 11: Lynx; pages 8 and 17 (left): Ardea; page 25: Robert Harding Library; pages 12 and 21 (inset): Survival Anglia: page 19 (top): Beauty Without Cruelty; page 22: Magnum; page 24: Panos; page 27: Philip Chapman.

PRINTED IN BELGIUM BY
proost
INTERNATIONAL BOOK PRODUCTION